The Comedy of Errors

Published by Sweet Cherry Publishing Limited
Unit 36, Vulcan House,
Vulcan Road,
Leicester, LE5 3EF
United Kingdom

First published in the US in 2013
2020 hardback edition

2 4 6 8 10 9 7 5 3 1

ISBN: 978-1-78226-670-9

© Macaw Books

The Comedy of Errors

Lexile® code numerical measure L = Lexile® 1060L

Cover design and illustrations by Macaw Books

www.sweetcherrypublishing.com

Printed and bound in India
I.TP002

~ About ~
Shakespeare

William Shakespeare, regarded as the greatest writer in the English language, was born in Stratford-upon-Avon in Warwickshire, England, in 1564. He was the third of eight children born to John and Mary Shakespeare.

Shakespeare was a poet, playwright and dramatist. He is often known as England's national poet and the "Bard of Avon." Thirty-eight plays, one hundred and fifty-four sonnets, two long narrative poems and several other poems are attributed to him. Shakespeare's plays have been translated into every major existent language and are performed more often than those of any other playwright.

Antipholus of Syracuse: He is the son of Aegon and identical twin brother of Antipholus of Ephesus. He has been searching for his brother for the last seven years. He is restless and anxious, and feels completely at a loss when he finds himself in strange situations.

Antipholus of Ephesus: He is the identical twin brother of Antipholus of Syracuse. He is a wealthy merchant in Ephesus and is married to Adriana. He is settled and well respected, but he too becomes a victim of the confusion in the play.

Adriana: She is the wife of Antipholus of Ephesus and sister of Luciana. She is a jealous woman by nature and thinks that her husband is cheating on her.

Dromio of Syracuse and Dromio of Ephesus: These two are identical twins like their masters. They are good-natured and witty. They too find themselves in strange situations because of their mistaken identities.

The Comedy of Errors

Once upon a time, there was great enmity brewing between the states of Ephesus and Syracuse. The levels of animosity had reached such a level that if a person from either state was seen in the

other state, he would be
executed immediately.

So one day, when Aegon,
an old merchant of Syracuse,
was found loitering aimlessly on
the streets of Ephesus, he was at
once apprehended and brought
before the king. The king showed

mercy and told him he must pay a fine—a rather huge sum—or else be executed.

Aegon had no money with him and he informed the king so. But before the king could tell his soldiers to take him away and kill him, Aegon begged that he be allowed to tell his story one last time. The king agreed, as he wanted to know why a merchant from Syracuse had dared to enter

Ephesus, knowing full well the consequences that he would face.

Aegon said that he was born in Syracuse and had become a successful merchant. In his youth, he had married a pretty girl. Soon after his marriage, he was forced to go to Epidamnum

on business. When he realized he was going to be delayed there, he at once sent for his wife. Shortly after her arrival, she gave birth to identical twin sons. As Aegon tried to come to terms with his own twins, the lady of the inn where they

11

had been staying died, leaving
behind two infant twin boys.
Feeling sorry for them, Aegon
took them in and raised them
as servants for his own sons.

However, his perils began
on his journey back to Syracuse.
Their ship encountered bad

weather, perhaps the worst storm
they had seen for quite some
time. Soon, the ship started to
capsize, and the captain, along
with the sailors, got into a
lifeboat and hurried away, leaving
Aegon, his wife, his sons and
the two other boys on the ship.

Not knowing what to do, Aegon tied his younger son and the younger servant to a mast and instructed his wife to do the same with the other two children. As soon as she had done so, the ship crashed against a huge rock and was split in two. While Aegon was able to drift away with the younger children, his wife held onto the mast with the elder ones.

While they were still battling
the waves, Aegon saw that some
fishermen had rescued his wife
and the two children. He was
happy that they were safe.

Some time later, some boats came to his rescue and were kind enough to let him get off at Syracuse. But from that moment on he was in the direst of troubles, as he could not find his wife, his elder son and the elder servant anywhere.

When
his younger
son turned
eighteen, he
decided to
leave in search
of his mother and brother,
accompanied by his servant,
who wanted to find his own

brother. Seven years passed, and for the last five, Aegon had traveled the world in search of his whole family. He had now arrived in Ephesus and knew this was going to be his last trip. He just wanted to know whether his family was safe; he had no fear of losing his own life.

The king was moved by this sad story. He told Aegon that it was not in his power to change the laws of the land, though he did want to spare his life. He gave Aegon leave for the day so that he could

try to borrow some money for
the fine and save himself.

Aegon thought that he was
doomed because he did not know
anyone in Ephesus who would
lend him such a high sum. Little
did he know that his younger
son, for whom he had been

looking for the
past five years,
was currently
in Ephesus, as
was his elder son,
whom he had not

seen since that fateful day at sea.

The two sons of Aegon, as

well as being
identical in
appearance,
were both called
Antipholus. The
same was true of
the two servant
brothers, who
were identical
and had the
name Dromio.

The day Aegon arrived in
Ephesus, Antipholus of Syracuse
and his Dromio also arrived in
the city. Knowing about the law
for people from Syracuse entering
Ephesus, they had pretended to
be merchants from Epidamnum.

Antipholus of Ephesus, the
elder son of Aegon, had had a
tough time since being rescued
by the fishermen that night. They
had taken the two children from
the hapless lady, intending to
sell them. After many ups and
downs, Antipholus of Ephesus

was now one of the richest merchants in the city. He lived there with his servant Dromio and his pretty wife, Adriana, a rich lady of Ephesus. He barely remembered his father and mother, for he had been very young when they were separated. He could have easily paid his father's fine if he had known that the man they had arrested

from Syracuse was
actually his father.

Antipholus
of Syracuse, who
had come in search
of his brother, was once again
roaming the streets. He sent his
Dromio to an inn where they
were to dine and decided to join

him after making some inquiries. But he knew that this was going to be a rather difficult task. He observed, "I am like a drop of water in the ocean, which, seeking to find its fellow drop, loses itself in the wide sea."

Suddenly, he saw Dromio walking towards him. Wondering why Dromio was not waiting for him at the inn, Antipholus of Syracuse walked up to him and asked him the reason for his haste. But Dromio replied

that he had been sent by the
mistress to call him for dinner.
Now Antipholus of Syracuse's
Dromio was often known to jest
with his master. After all, they
had grown up more as brothers
than as master and servant.
But Antipholus of Syracuse
felt this was a little too much
and completely uncalled for.

Dromio kept insisting that his wife had asked him to come home and join her and her sister for dinner. Antipholus of Syracuse kept repeating that he

29

had no wife and ordered Dromio
to stop joking. But when Dromio
said he did not understand what
his master was saying, Antipholus
of Syracuse beat him. Dromio
ran straight home to the house
of Antipholus of Ephesus, for
he was the other Dromio, and

told his mistress that his master
had refused to come and had
said that he had no wife.

This made Adriana mad
and she was full of jealousy. Her
sister, Luciana, who lived in
the same house, tried her best

to calm her, but
Adriana was
in no mood
to listen.

Meanwhile,
Antipholus of
Syracuse had returned
to the inn and found Dromio
sitting there waiting for him.
Just as he was about
to chide Dromio
for his silly jest,
Adriana came
before him and
asked him why he
had refused to come
home. Antipholus
tried to explain to
her that he had not

come home because he did not
have a home here, which only
angered Adriana even more. She
was furious with Antipholus for
refusing to recognize his own
wife. Unable to calm Adriana,
Antipholus of Syracuse was
forced to go over to his brother's
house and have dinner with

his wife and sister-in-law, along
with his Dromio. Antipholus
of Syracuse now started to
wonder whether he had been
married in his sleep, or whether
he was sleeping right now.

Meanwhile, Antipholus of
Ephesus had found Dromio and
had gone home with him for
dinner. But Adriana had given
strict orders to the servants not
to admit anyone while they were

eating. So when Antipholus and
Dromio arrived and knocked on
the door, the servants refused to
let them in. After many attempts,
Antipholus walked off in a huff,
enraged that his wife was having
dinner with another man.

As soon as Antipholus of Syracuse finished his dinner, he decided to run away from the madhouse. He liked Luciana, but the ill-tempered Adriana frightened him. He also learned that Dromio had been taken

away by his own wife, though
he had never known Dromio
to be married. Master and
servant were more than happy
to find an excuse to leave.

On the road, he was
summoned by a goldsmith who
gave him a chain. Antipholus

declared that the chain was not
his, but the goldsmith insisted
that it had been made on his
special orders, and leaving
the chain in his hand, he left.
Antipholus immediately asked
Dromio to arrange for a passage
out of the city, for he did not
want to stay there any longer.

Moments later, the
goldsmith was arrested for the
non-payment of a debt he owed.
He suddenly spied Antipholus
of Ephesus walking
towards him and
asked him to
pay the price of
the chain, a sum

that was almost the same as the amount he had borrowed. But Antipholus insisted that he had never received a chain from the goldsmith, while the goldsmith was adamant that he had given him the chain personally.

Due to this argument, the goldsmith and Antipholus were arrested immediately.

As he was being taken to jail, Antipholus met Dromio of Syracuse, who was coming to tell his master that the departure from the city had been arranged. But Antipholus, mistaking him for his own Dromio, asked him to go home and get the money for the fine from his wife. Dromio did not understand why his master wanted him to go back to the same house from which they had barely managed to escape earlier, but being the obedient servant he was, he left immediately.

Adriana gave him the money, and when Dromio was returning, he saw Antipholus of Syracuse being measured by a tailor who insisted on making him new clothes. Antipholus of

45

Ephesus was clearly a well-known man in the city.

Dromio could not understand how his master had freed himself from his captors and asked him to explain. He told him he had managed to acquire the money for his release from Adriana. Antipholus of

Syracuse now thought that someone had put a spell on them.

While he was still wondering what to do, a lady walked up to him and reminded him about the gold chain he was supposed to have given her. When Antipholus denied knowing the woman,

she mentioned that if he would not give her the chain as he had promised, he should at least give her back the ring she had given him. Unable to bear it any longer, Antipholus started screaming and ran away.

The lady whom Antipholus of Ephesus had actually dined with and to whom he had indeed promised the gold chain, went to Adriana and explained that her husband had gone mad. Then Antipholus entered, attended by a jailer. He had been allowed to come

home and take the money for
his own release, as Dromio
had clearly not reached him.
But Adriana assured him that
she had sent Dromio with
the money a while ago.

Adriana and Antipholus
started fighting about the
woman, and Antipholus tried

to remind her that she had not
let him come home for dinner
the night before.
Adriana reminded
Antipholus that he
had protested that
she was not his
wife. Antipholus
obviously denied

this, and Adriana was now convinced that her husband had gone mad. She made the servants tie him up while she went to get a doctor.

When Adriana left, she found Antipholus and Dromio walking around outside the convent. Thinking that her husband had managed to escape,

she and her sister Luciana attempted to restrain him again. Seeing Adriana charging towards them, Antipholus and Dromio ran into the convent and took shelter.

The lady abbess came out to inquire about the reason for the pursuit of

the two men and Adriana told
her all that had happened. The
lady abbess wanted to find out
the true reason for Antipholus
going mad, but unable to get a
satisfactory answer, she was not
convinced. But when Adriana
told her that she believed he was
in love with another woman and
kept reprimanding him

for it, the abbess came to the conclusion that it was Adriana's jealous temper that had made her husband mad. Adriana then started to believe that it was all her fault.

Meanwhile, Aegon's time was coming to an end. He was to be executed at the end of the

day at a place just
behind the convent.
The king had
come along in the
event that someone
might pay the fine
for old Aegon and he could be
pardoned. But just as the king
approached the convent, Adriana

came over to him, wailing
that the abbess was not letting
her take her mad husband.

While she was crying,
Antipholus of Ephesus and his
servant, who had managed to
escape, came running over to
them and declared that his evil
wife had locked him up and
declared him to be a lunatic.

On seeing Antipholus, his
lost son, after seven years, Aegon
was overjoyed. He knew that
his son would at once pay the
sum for his release and requested
Antipholus to do it. But to his
surprise, his son completely
denied knowing him. He
declared that he had never seen
the old man in his life, and was

surely not going to pay the fine. While this state of madness was going on outside, the lady abbess, along with Antipholus and Dromio of Syracuse, turned up to see what all the commotion was about. But if Adriana was talking to her husband and servant outside, then who were these two men?

Finally, the mystery was solved. The king, who had heard Aegon's story earlier, immediately realized what was going on. He declared that these were the twin

sons of Aegon and the twin
servants he had spoken about.

When the king concluded,
the lady abbess gave a small cry
and said that she was indeed the
wife of Aegon, from whom her
sons had been taken away that
fateful night. She had joined
a nunnery and, through her

devoted service, had taken the rank of abbess at the convent.

Everything was finally wound up. Antipholus of Ephesus had wanted to pay his father's fine immediately, but the king pardoned Aegon without the need for any payment. He was very happy to see the entire family

reunited. Even the Dromios were overjoyed at seeing each other again.

Adriana had learned a lesson from the abbess, her mother-in-law, and never raised any more suspicions about her husband's character. Antipholus of Syracuse married the fair Luciana and together they all lived happily in Ephesus for the rest of their lives.